DAVID SMALL

Eulalie and the Hopping Head

A Sunburst Book • Farrar Straus Giroux

For Sarah

Copyright © 1982 by David Small
All rights reserved
Distributed in Canada by Douglas & McIntyre Ltd.
Printed and bound in the United States of America by Berryville Graphics
First published by Macmillan Publishing Co., Inc., 1982
First Farrar, Straus and Giroux edition, 2001
First Sunburst edition, 2001
1 3 5 7 9 10 8 6 4 2

Library of Congress Cataloging-in-Publication Data
Small, David, 1945–
   Eulalie and the hopping head / David Small.—1st Farrar, Straus and Giroux ed.
   p. cm.
   Summary: An abandoned doll, who seems to be a perfect child, can't compare with a toad's
own beloved, but imperfect daughter.
   ISBN 0-374-42202-8 (pbk.)
   [1. Toads—Fiction. 2. Dolls—Fiction. 3. Parent and child—Fiction.] I. Title.

PZ7.S638 Eu 2001
[E]—dc21
                                                                    00-62227

It was a bright spring day, and Mother Lumps and her daughter, Eulalie, were out for their daily stroll. Sometimes Eulalie walked, but most of all she liked to ride.

"Why, there's Mrs. Shinn," said Mother Lumps. She knew Mrs. Shinn only slightly but had long admired her for her beautiful bushy tail.

"Let me see that child!" said Mrs. Shinn eagerly, peering into the carriage.

"Is she good?" asked Mrs. Shinn.

"Oh!" said Mother Lumps. "Eulalie is a wonderful child."

"Then of course she has very good manners," said the stylish fox, "and is very clean and quiet."

"Well," said Mother Lumps, "Eulalie is not all grown up, so her manners are not yet perfect. Like all children, she is sometimes messy, and she does cry at times."

Mrs. Shinn looked down at Mother Lumps with a dark expression. "I have nine children," she growled. "Each one of them is perfect. I taught them to behave properly from the day they were born!"

They came to an old apple grove and paused to rest in the shade. Mother Lumps reached over to pat Eulalie on the head.

"Look there," said Mrs. Shinn. "Talk about perfect children—there is a child that any mother would be proud of!"

Mother Lumps and Eulalie looked and saw a child resting against a tree trunk. She did not move and said not a word.

"What is this child doing out here alone?" asked Mother Lumps.

"It's been here for days," said Mrs. Shinn in low tones. "It was left here during a picnic and no one has come back for it."

"Then she has been abandoned!" cried Mother Lumps. "She has no one to care for her."

Mrs. Shinn sighed. "Yes, and a pity, too. I would take her home myself, but with nine other children there's no room. This is a well-mannered child and quiet . . . so quiet! I've spoken to her several times, but she is so shy she never says a word. You should take her home with you."

Mother Lumps bent close to the child. "I wonder what she eats," she said. "She must be very hungry by now."

Mrs. Shinn laughed gaily. "Fortunately for you, I've never seen this child eat a thing. You'll never have to feed her. What's more, she never gets dirty, as she is always careful to stay in one place. Come along, I'll help you take her home."

"Well, of course," Mother Lumps said, a little uncertainly. "We can't just leave her here." Together they raised the child to her feet.

"Come now, dear," said Mother Lumps to the child. "You're much too big for the carriage. You'll have to walk."

The child did not move, and Mother Lumps had to drag her as she pushed Eulalie's carriage.

As they walked, Eulalie leaned over and told the child, "You really ought to stand up. You'll get your dress dirty that way."

The child said nothing, but Mrs. Shinn immediately replied, "I told you. This child makes no noise. Because of that it is better than all other children. *Your* child, Mother Lumps, would do well to follow its example!"

Just then, the child's head fell off and rolled into the grass.
Mrs. Shinn quickly picked it up, dusted it carelessly with
her handkerchief, and put it back on.

"Well," she said, "perhaps this child is not quite perfect."
Eulalie and Mother Lumps peered anxiously into the child's
face and saw that, in spite of the accident, she smiled as always.

On the way home, the child's head fell off six more times. Eulalie laughed each time this happened. She thought it was a fine, funny trick!

At last they reached the cottage, and Mother Lumps invited Mrs. Shinn to tea. When Mother Lumps passed the cookies, Eulalie took two and offered one to the new child, who took not one bite or even said thank you.

It was now quite late. Mrs. Shinn said her goodbyes and went home.

The next morning, Mother Lumps decided to take the children out for a stroll. Eulalie was already dressed and playing outside, and Mother Lumps began to get the new child ready to go.

As the child refused to walk and was much too large to fit in the carriage, Mother Lumps decided to take along only its head. By itself, the head was just the right size.

"Now," said Mother Lumps, "where's Eulalie?" And she went out to find her.

A few minutes later, Eulalie came inside. She looked about for her mother and saw her carriage standing by the open door. "Oh, good!" she said. "We're going for a ride!" Eulalie climbed up and found herself looking into the child's face.

"Hello!" said Eulalie.

The child did not answer.

Then Eulalie noticed that the head was hollow, and climbed inside. It was a tight fit, but there was enough room to move around, and Eulalie discovered she could see out through the large glass eyes.

Mother Lumps returned. She was certain Eulalie was playing somewhere in the garden, so she decided to take the new child and look for her. As soon as the carriage was wheeled out into the sunshine, Eulalie began talking, her voice coming through the mouth of the head. "Oh, Mama!" she said. "Isn't it a pretty day?"

Mother Lumps jumped with surprise and then sighed with relief.

"Well," she said, "now that you've started to talk you'll surely want something to eat."

"Oh, yes. Please," said Eulalie.

"How about a nice worm?" asked Mother Lumps. She plucked a fat earthworm from the ground and dropped it into the head's mouth.

Inside, Eulalie took the worm, gobbled it up, and said, "Yum!"

"Well now," Mother Lumps said happily, "do you want
something to drink?"

"Yes, please. I'm thirsty!" cried the tiny voice.

Mother Lumps found a walnut shell full of rainwater and
raised it to the child's mouth.

The water poured in, and Eulalie screamed.

"Stop, Mother! Help! Enough!" Eulalie coughed and sputtered and wiggled and squirmed. She tried to squeeze out of the head, but all she could manage to get out was her legs.

Mother Lumps gasped when she saw the child's head stand up on two little legs and jump into the air. Then the head began to hop around the garden.

At that moment, Mrs. Shinn appeared. "Good afternoon," she called. "And how is that perfect new child today?"

"She's run away!" cried Mother Lumps.

"What?" said Mrs. Shinn. "Impossible! She's a perfect child."

"It's true," said Mother Lumps. "She hopped off. I can't find her anywhere!"

"You've gone mad," said Mrs. Shinn. "That child would do no such thing. That's the beauty of her, after all—no trouble to the mother."

"But she is gone!" wailed Mother Lumps as she frantically searched the garden.

Suddenly the head leaped out from under a clump of toadflax.

"There she is!" screamed Mother Lumps.

With one hop, the head was on top of the gate, and with another, it was in the arms of Mrs. Shinn.

Mrs. Shinn stumbled and fell into a puddle of mud.
She slipped and splashed about and then, with an outraged
bark, ran down the road, disappearing into the forest.

The head fell to the ground and came up with a thud against
a large rock. Out popped Eulalie!

Mother Lumps rushed to pick her up.

"Oh, Mama," Eulalie said happily, "it was so much fun! But then there was so much water and I couldn't see you, and then there was lots of noise and rolling around and a big bump . . . and here you are!"

Mother Lumps carried Eulalie inside and wrapped her snugly in a quilt, kissing her each time she made a tuck, while laughing at her own foolishness.

Forever after, the new child—its head securely fastened—sat in a chair and did nothing while Eulalie ran and sang and played. And to anyone who asked, Mother Lumps replied, "I have two children. One is perfect and is no trouble to its mother. The other one is sometimes noisy and often forgets to clean up after herself, but I love her a thousand times more!"

Everyone understood this, even Mrs. Shinn.